# SIX QUEENS, ONE KING

## THE EXTRAORDINARY REIGN OF HENRY VIII

Written by Kay Barnham

Illustrated by Giorgio Bacchin

## CONTENTS

## Collins

T0321635

# 1 TUDOR MONARCHS

Today, the British **monarch**'s role is to represent their country and to perform official duties. Meanwhile, a government is elected by the population to run the country. But it hasn't *always* been this way.

When the Tudors reigned, from 1485 to 1603, the monarch was in charge of *everything*. No one voted for them. They ruled simply because they had **inherited** the throne or had won it in battle, like Henry VII, the first Tudor king.

Tudor monarchs had plenty of friends, keen to support them and share in their success. But there were rivals too, eager to seize the throne for themselves. Kings and queens had to be on their guard at all times. And if a royal family wanted to stay in power, there was one thing a monarch needed – an **heir** …

When there has been more than one king or queen with the same name we use Roman numerals after their name.

| 1 | 2 | 3 | 4 | 5 | 6 | 7 | 8 | 9 | 10 |
|---|---|---|---|---|---|---|---|---|---|
| I | II | III | IV | V | VI | VII | VIII | IX | X |

So Henry VIII was Henry the Eighth!

3

When Henry Tudor was born in 1491, no one expected him ever to be crowned King of England. His older brother Arthur was already heir to the English throne. Whenever their father – Henry VII – died, Arthur would be the next king, not Henry.

So Arthur had a solid royal training. At the age of 15, he was married to a Spanish princess named Catherine of Aragon. And then the unthinkable happened – Arthur died.

Henry was just ten years old. He had no idea how to be king when his father died.

Seven years later, in 1509, he would find out.

## Top Tudor fact

**Jousting** was strictly prohibited for Henry when he was a child. It was far too dangerous for the heir to the throne. But as the new king, Henry VIII could do as he liked. And he was a fan of jousting for the rest of his life!

# 2 THE YOUNG KING

One of the first things 17-year-old Henry VIII did was to marry his brother's widow. This was not an unusual thing to happen. Catherine of Aragon's first marriage to Arthur had cemented the relationship between England and Spain. Her marriage to Henry made sure that the two countries remained **allies**.

Crowds gathered to celebrate the coronation of the new king and queen. But, just two days later, Henry VIII gave the public a first glimpse of his darker side, when he threw Edmund Dudley and Sir Richard Empson in prison. These men had worked for Henry VII and carried out the old king's unpopular orders.

Henry VIII wanted to show everyone that he wasn't like his father. He was fair.

So he had Dudley and Empson beheaded.

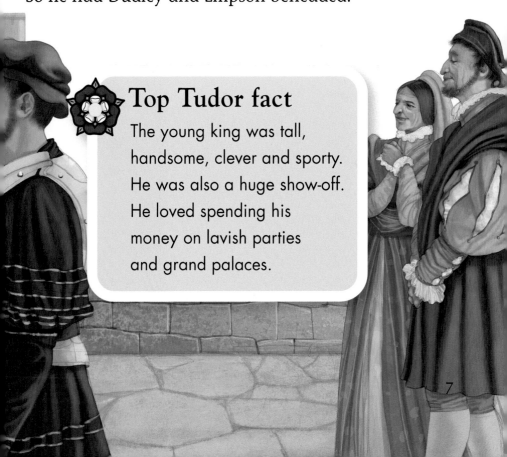

## Top Tudor fact

The young king was tall, handsome, clever and sporty. He was also a huge show-off. He loved spending his money on lavish parties and grand palaces.

Six years after she married the king, Catherine of Aragon gave birth. Henry VIII had a royal heir! The bad news was that the baby was a girl. Her name was Mary.

A Tudor queen was *not* part of Henry VIII's plan. There had been no ruling queens of England so far and it was impossible to predict what would happen if a woman were on the throne. Would she be up to the job? What if others challenged her, simply because she was female? To be certain that the Tudor royal family would survive, Henry believed he needed a son to rule after him.

But, as the years went by, it became increasingly unlikely that he and Catherine would have any more children. A male heir was now out of the question.

Or was it …?

# 3 THE CATHOLIC CHURCH

In 1527, Henry decided that he didn't have a son because his marriage to Catherine of Aragon had been doomed from the start. He should never have married his brother's widow. And the Pope should never have allowed the marriage to happen.

## Top Tudor fact

At the beginning of the 16th century, England was a Catholic country. The Pope was in charge of the Catholic Church, not the monarch.

Now, to set things right, Henry VIII wanted to divorce Catherine of Aragon. This would leave him free to marry again. As divorce wasn't allowed, he asked Pope Clement VII to make an exception. But the Pope refused Henry's request. He told the king that if he remarried, he would be thrown out of the Catholic Church.

# 4 THE CHURCH OF ENGLAND

Thomas Cromwell – one of the king's top advisors – spent years trying to persuade the Pope that Henry VIII's first marriage should never have taken place. (This was because of an ancient law that said it was illegal to marry a brother- or sister-in-law.) But the Pope stood firm.

Cromwell's next plan was more ambitious: why shouldn't Henry VIII start a new church? If the English monarch were the head of that church, then they could make their own decisions. They wouldn't need the Pope's approval.

So plans to create the Church of England were made. Meanwhile, it was declared that Henry's marriage to Catherine of Aragon had never been valid.

13

# THE LOWDOWN ON ...

## CATHERINE OF ARAGON

Henry VIII's first wife

**Name:** Catherine of Aragon

**Born:** 16th December 1485

**Died:** 7th January 1536

**Place of birth:** Alcalá de Henares, Spain

**Married to Henry VIII:**
11th June 1509-23rd May 1533

**Children:** Mary I

Catherine of Aragon was the youngest child of two Spanish monarchs - Isabella I of Castile and Ferdinand II of Aragon. Her parents paid for Italian explorer Christopher Columbus's first voyage across the Atlantic Ocean in 1492.

When she married Henry VIII, Catherine was 23 - six years older than the new king.

Catherine's marriage to Henry VIII lasted more than twice as long as all of his other marriages put together! She was his wife for almost 24 years.

Catherine was a **staunch** Catholic. Her divorce from Henry VIII was totally against her wishes.

# 5 A CORONATION FIT FOR A QUEEN

Now Henry VIII could marry whoever he liked …
and he knew the very woman! The king had admired
Anne Boleyn for years. She was clever, musical
and very stylish.

His new wife's coronation was spectacular and lasted
for four days. Henry VIII and Anne Boleyn were rowed
along the River Thames, their royal barge at the centre
of a colourful **flotilla**. They arrived at the Tower of
London to the sound of cannon fire.

Two days later, Anne Boleyn took part in
a magnificent procession through streets hung with
decorations and lined with people. The next day at
Westminster Abbey, she was officially crowned Queen
of England.

There was a good reason why Henry VIII had planned
such a glorious coronation for his new wife. He was
thrilled that Anne Boleyn was already expecting
a child. And he was sure that it was a boy.

The royal baby arrived in September 1533. But instead of the boy Henry VIII longed for, it was another girl. The new princess was named Elizabeth.

The king was devastated. After everything he'd done to marry Anne Boleyn, he was still no further forward in his quest for a male heir.

The royal couple hoped that a baby boy would swiftly follow. But two years passed and a son didn't arrive. By now, Henry was 44 years old and time was running out. He couldn't bear the idea that he might die without a male heir. He needed to do something ... and fast.

## Top Tudor fact

Henry VIII planned a great joust to celebrate the arrival of his son. When a healthy daughter was born instead, the joust was cancelled.

# 6 A NEW LOVE

Henry VIII turned his attention away from the queen and towards another member of the **royal court**. She was Anne Boleyn's **lady-in-waiting** and her name was Jane Seymour.

Jane was quite different to Henry VIII's first two wives. She wasn't as highly educated – she could read and write only a little – and she wasn't lively and outspoken either.

Anne Boleyn was furious that Henry VIII was spending more time with her lady-in-waiting than he was with his own wife. But the king had already ended one marriage. There was nothing to stop him from doing it again.

## Top Tudor fact

In 1536, after a serious jousting accident, Henry was unconscious for two hours. If he suffered a head injury, this may explain why his behaviour was so extreme from then on.

# 7 BEHEADED!

Henry VIII claimed to have proof that Anne Boleyn had broken the law and been involved with other men. The queen was arrested and imprisoned in the Tower of London. Few people were ready to help her – especially when it meant siding against the powerful king – and she was found guilty of crimes including witchcraft and **high treason**. The punishment was death.

On 19th May 1536, Anne Boleyn was taken to Tower Green, where her head was sliced off with one stroke.

Henry VIII's second wife was dead.

## Top Tudor fact

Henry VIII ordered thousands of people to be hanged, burnt to death, boiled alive or beheaded. The usual way of beheading someone was with an axe – a clumsy way of killing. But the king sent for a skilful French swordsman to chop off Anne's head.

# THE LOWDOWN ON ...

## ANNE BOLEYN

Henry VIII's second wife

**Name:** Anne Boleyn

**Born:** sometime between 1501 and 1507

**Died:** 19th May 1536

**Place of birth:** Norfolk or Kent, England

**Married to Henry VIII:**
28th May 1533-14th May 1536

**Children:** Elizabeth I

Anne Boleyn was the daughter of Sir Thomas Boleyn and Lady Elizabeth Howard, who later became an earl and a countess.

Anne spent her youth serving in royal courts in the Netherlands and France, before becoming a lady-in-waiting for Henry VIII's first wife.

Thanks to her time spent abroad, Anne was fluent in French. She was also cultured, highly educated and wore the very latest French fashions.

Henry VIII married Anne before his marriage to Catherine of Aragon had officially ended.

Anne was the second of Henry's wives to have a coronation ... and the last.

# 8 A SON, AT LAST!

The day after Anne Boleyn was beheaded, 44-year-old Henry VIII became **betrothed** to Jane Seymour. Ten days after that, he married her.

Jane Seymour was a strict, serious queen, who insisted that everyone serving at the royal court was on their best behaviour. She also persuaded the king that his first daughter Mary should join the royal household.

By the following year, Jane was pregnant. On 12th October 1537, a royal prince was born. He was named Edward. At last, Henry VIII had the male heir he'd wanted for so long. But 12 days later, the queen died. The king was heartbroken.

Jane Seymour was the only one of Henry VIII's wives to be given a state funeral. He said she was his favourite.

# THE LOWDOWN ON ...

## JANE SEYMOUR

### Henry VIII's third wife

**Name:** Jane Seymour

**Born:** between 1504 and 1509

**Died:** 24th October 1537

**Place of birth:** probably Wolf Hall, Wiltshire, England

**Married to Henry VIII:**
30th May 1536–24th October 1537

**Children:** Edward VI

Jane Seymour came from a wealthy and important family. Her father, Sir John Seymour, was a soldier and **courtier** for both Henry VII and Henry VIII. This made it easy for Jane to get a job at the royal court.

Jane wasn't just Anne Boleyn's lady-in-waiting – she was her second cousin, too.

Quiet and shy, Jane was highly skilled at needlework.

Jane was never crowned. This could be because coronations were very expensive. Or it might be because a **plague** meant large events could not take place at that time. Or perhaps Henry VIII wanted Jane to prove herself by having a son first. No one knows for sure.

# 9 A POLITICAL MATCH

It would be two years before Henry VIII married again.
This time, he didn't marry for love. Thomas Cromwell
was worried that England was in danger of attack.
But if the king formed a new alliance – by marrying
someone from another country – England would
be safer. Anne of Cleves was the sister of a
German duke. She was the perfect match.

The royal couple met for the first time just five days before their wedding. It was *not* love at first sight. And it was too late to back out …

Six months later, the marriage was **annulled**. Henry VIII gave Anne of Cleves two royal properties and an allowance. Thomas Cromwell wasn't so lucky. As punishment for persuading the king that the marriage was a good idea, he was beheaded.

## Top Tudor fact

Because of his very unhealthy diet, Henry VIII spent a lot of time sitting on the toilet. The groom of the stool was a man employed to keep him company … and wipe his bottom too!

# THE LOWDOWN ON ...

## ANNE OF CLEVES

Henry VIII's fourth wife

**Name:** Anne of Cleves

**Born:** 22nd September 1515

**Died:** 16th July 1557

**Place of birth:** Düsseldorf, present-day Germany

**Married to Henry VIII:**
6th January 1540–9th July 1540

**Children:** None

Anne of Cleves was the daughter of John III, Duke of Cleves - a member of the German **aristocracy**.

Before meeting Henry VIII, Anne was painted by German artist Hans Holbein the Younger. It's rumoured that she wasn't quite as beautiful as her portrait.

When she married Henry VIII, Anne was 24 years old - exactly half the king's age.

Henry VIII and Anne were married for just six months and three days. It was the shortest of all six of the king's marriages.

Anne outlived Henry VIII and all of his other wives.

# 10 THE YOUNGEST QUEEN

By the time his marriage to Anne of Cleves had ended, Henry VIII had already fallen in love with one of her ladies-in-waiting. Catherine Howard was young, happy and lively. This time, the king decided that he would not let others pick a wife for him. He was 49, but his fifth wife was probably a teenager.

At first, things went well. But then rumours began to spread around the royal court that Catherine had been seeing other men. Henry was furious. He decided that his wife should no longer be Queen of England. So Catherine Howard lost her title. Three months later, she also lost her head.

## Top Tudor fact

Henry VIII was very fit when he was young, but as he grew older, his health worsened. He suffered from painful leg ulcers, which may have contributed to his bad temper.

# THE LOWDOWN ON ...

## CATHERINE HOWARD

Henry VIII's fifth wife

**Name:** Catherine Howard

**Born:** between 1518 and 1525

**Died:** 13th February 1542

**Place of birth:** London

**Married to Henry VIII:**
28th July 1540 - 13th February 1542

**Children:** None

Catherine Howard was one of ten children.
Her father was a lord, but her uncle was a duke
and a Tudor politician. It was he who made it possible
for Catherine to serve at the royal court.

Catherine was Anne Boleyn's cousin and Jane Seymour's
second cousin.

Unlike Anne Boleyn, who was beheaded with a sword,
Catherine's executioner used an axe.

Catherine was the youngest of Henry's wives. Her date
of birth is unknown, but she may have been just
17 when she was beheaded.

# 11 THE LAST QUEEN

After a lifetime of sporting injuries and unhealthy living, by the time he was 52, Henry VIII was very unwell. But his poor health didn't stop him from marrying yet again.

Catherine Parr became the king's sixth wife. Twice widowed, she was well educated and could speak many languages. She was perhaps the luckiest of Henry VIII's queens. She was neither divorced nor beheaded. Instead, she outlived the king.

Henry VIII died on 28th January 1547. He chose to be buried beside Jane Seymour. Of all his wives, she had given him what he wanted most in all the world – a male heir.

## Top Tudor fact

When he was older, Henry VIII was so overweight that he was carried upstairs and downstairs by chair. He even had to be hoisted on to his horse!

# THE LOWDOWN ON ...

## CATHERINE PARR

Henry VIII's sixth wife

**Name:** Catherine Parr

**Born:** 1512

**Died:** 5th September 1548

**Place of birth:** London

**Married to Henry VIII:**
12th July 1543 – 28th January 1547

**Children:** Mary Seymour

Catherine Parr came from a respected family from the north of England. Her father was Sir Thomas Parr, a friend of Henry VIII.

Her godmother was Catherine of Aragon. Catherine Parr may have been named after her.

Catherine wrote and published three books.

Twice widowed before she wed Henry VIII, Catherine was married four times in total. She had more husbands than any other queen of England.

Catherine married Sir Thomas Seymour (Jane Seymour's brother) after the king's death. She died after giving birth to their daughter.

Henry VIII's son – Edward VI – was crowned when he was nine years old, but he died just six years later.

Henry's eldest daughter reigned next. Mary I was a strict Catholic and became known as Bloody Mary after executing hundreds of people who didn't share her religious beliefs. Curiously, Henry VIII was never given such a nickname, despite the fact that he was responsible for the deaths of tens of thousands of people. After five years as queen, Mary I died.

Finally, Elizabeth I was crowned queen. Henry VIII might have feared that a female heir was a ridiculous idea, but his daughter proved him wrong. A strong, firm ruler, she was so popular that she became known as Good Queen Bess. Her 44-year reign was named the Elizabethan Era. She was the last of the Tudors.

In 2011, the Royal Equality Act made it law that a British king or queen's oldest child became heir, no matter what their gender.

# GLOSSARY

**allies** people or countries who fight together

**annulled** when it is announced that something does not legally exist

**aristocracy** people who have usually inherited titles such as earl, countess, king or queen

**betrothed** engaged to be married

**courtier** a person at a royal court who provides advice or companionship to the king or queen

**flotilla** a small fleet of boats or ships

**heir** someone who inherits money or a title after the current owner's death

**high treason** betraying the monarch

**inherited** money, property or a title that is given to an heir after someone dies

**jousting** a competition popular during the Middle Ages, in which knights on horseback charged at each other, both trying to knock off their opponent with a long stick called a lance

**lady-in-waiting** a woman who looks after a queen or
  princess and keeps them company

**monarch** an unelected head of a country, such as
  a king or queen

**plague** a deadly illness that infects lots of people very
  quickly

**royal court** all the people who live and work at
  the monarch's place of residence

**staunch** very loyal or firm

# HENRY VIII, HIS SIX WIVES AND THREE HEIRS

### CATHERINE OF ARAGON
Married 1509
Divorced 1533

### ANNE BOLEYN
Married 1533
Beheaded 1536

### JANE SEYMOUR
Married 1536
Died 1537

## MARY I
Reigned: 1553–1558

## ELIZABETH I
Reigned: 1558–1603

## EDWARD VI
Reigned: 1547–1553

# HENRY VIII
## Reigned: 1509–1547

**ANNE OF CLEVES**
Married 1540
Divorced 1540

**CATHERINE HOWARD**
Married 1540
Beheaded 1542

**CATHERINE PARR**
Married 1543
Survived

#  Ideas for reading

Written by Gill Matthews
*Primary Literacy Consultant*

**Reading objectives:**
- Read books that are structured in different ways and read for a range of purposes
- Retrieve, record and present information from non-fiction

**Spoken language objectives:**
- Give well-structured descriptions, explanations and narratives for different purposes, including for expressing feelings
- Participate in discussion, presentations, performances, role play, improvisations and debates

**Curriculum links:** History – a study of an aspect or theme in British history that extends pupils' chronological knowledge beyond 1066

**Interest words:** elected, reigned, inherited, crowned

## Build a context for reading
- Show the front cover and ask children what they see. Read the title. Ask what sort of book they think this is and how it might be organised.
- Ask children to read the back cover blurb. Explore existing knowledge about Henry VIII.
- Encourage children to develop three questions that they would like to find the answers to in the book. Discuss what strategies they could use to look for answers.

## Understand and apply reading strategies
- Read pp2–5. Ask whether children found anything surprising in this chapter.
- Ask children to turn to pp6–7. Demonstrate how to find information quickly by formulating a question, e.g. Who did Henry throw into prison? To find the answer, you are scanning for names. Give children another question which is answered on pp8–9 and ask them to scan to find the answer.